THE HOLE IN THE OCEAN

A DARING JOURNEY
Words and Pictures by Jasper Tomkins

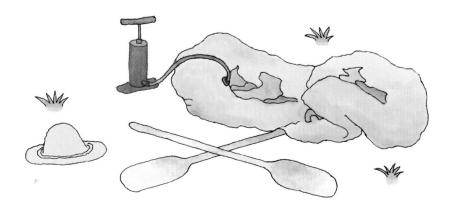

GREEN TIGER PRESS

Green Tiger Press

First Edition
ISBN 0-914676-73-3

Manufactured in Hong Kong
11 13 15 17 19 20 18 16 14 12

For the dream that lives within the sea.
A gift to the King of the Fishpeople.

Today is the day that we head out to sea,
Down to the dock, just you and just me.

Now step in lightly and then we'll leave.
I'll tell you a secret you'll never believe.

There's a hole in the ocean where everything goes,
And this hole is deeper than anyone knows.

I saw it in a dream one night;
I'll never forget that amazing sight.

A little bit farther and then you'll see
This wonder I speak of, this hole in the sea.

There it is! There it is! The hole's been found!
Out where the waves are circling 'round!

We've come much too close. We're about to go under.
Quick! Paddle harder! Can we make it, I wonder?

It's grabbing us up with an ocean-size kiss
And taking us down to see all the fish.

And now we're spinning down into the sea.
Hey—I'm awfully glad that you're here with me!

We've just passed a tree and a department store.
There goes an elephant riding a door.

Down go the ships and down go the houses.
Down go the birds and down go the mouses.

Look at the bugs and the jumping toads,
More and more cars and endless roads.

Good-bye flowers and fresh green grass
Bicycles, barbells, deep-sea bass...

Fuzzy caterpillars and long striped snakes,
Tall silver lampposts and white snowflakes.

Here is an octopus grabbing up cats.
Now, look here, we tell him, you can't take our hats.

Round and round we spiral down
I think we soon shall hit the ground.

But there are whales to see and a dog to catch.
Look out for that couch! Now the boat needs a patch!

We're spinning round faster—please hold my hand.
With a squish! And a bump! We've now hit the sand!

So this is the bottom, the ocean floor.
What! All of the buildings are just as before!

I see shoes and dogs, and there's Mr. Jones.
Look, here's the place with ice cream cones.

How completely at home everybody behaves.
Do you think that they notice they're under the waves?

Here is the park with the beautiful trees.
There are the flowers that make me sneeze.

This is my house and this is my street.
That *must* be my mother—she looks so sweet.

So how can this be? It doesn't make sense.
We can't be in the ocean—here's my cat on the fence.

I run up the steps and start to go in.
Mother's there, saying, "Where have you been?"

"I've been walking along on the floor of the sea.
But how can you be down here with me?"

"Now don't be silly or I'll send you to bed.
Come and eat dinner with me and Uncle Fred.

"Just remember to wash your hands.
And after dinner please clean the pans."

"Oh hum!" I say. "That's no way to act.
We've had an adventure, and that's a fact!"

"I'm tired and sleepy and I really need to rest.
But hey! Look at this! There's a fish in my vest!"

I'll never understand it, but what can I do?
No one else knows the secret—just we two.

There's a hole in the ocean, in the middle of the sea.
You really would believe it, if you'd only been me.

I've been there myself and it's very, very blue...